DISNEY

CAMP ROCK

SECOND SESSION #6

Sound Off!

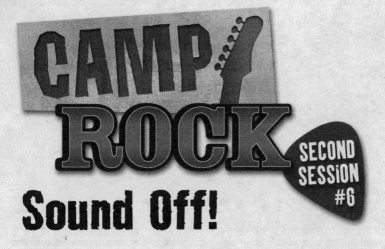

Sound Off!

By James Ponti

Based on "Camp Rock," Written by Karin Gist & Regina Hicks and Julie Brown & Paul Brown

Disney PRESS

New York

Library of Congress Catalog Card Number on file
ISBN 978-1-4231-1776-6

For more Disney Press fun, visit www.disneybooks.com
Visit DisneyChannel.com

CHAPTER ONE

Mitchie Torres was not a morning person. It didn't matter if she was at home during the school year or at Camp Rock in the summer, her goal was to get up at the last possible moment. The fact that musicians usually performed at night and slept late was part of the appeal of a life in rock and roll. But this morning, the piercing sound of an alarm clock was making sleep all but impossible.

At least it was for Mitchie.

On the other side of the cabin, her best friend, Caitlyn Gellar, was sleeping like a baby, completely unaffected by the alarm's buzz.

Mitchie attempted to block out the sound by wrapping a pillow around her head. When that didn't work, she tried a blanket. Out of frustration, she chucked the pillow across the room and hit Caitlyn right in the head. If she was going to suffer, she at least wanted to suffer with company.

But Caitlyn just took a swat at the pillow as if it were a mosquito and rolled over, all without giving the slightest sign of waking up.

Finally, brushing her brown bangs out of her eyes, Mitchie got up and walked over to Caitlyn's nightstand. Making as much noise as she could, she turned off the alarm.

"Wake up!" Mitchie cried, shaking her friend by the shoulder. "It's the least you can do, considering it's *your* alarm clock going off."

Caitlyn was even less of a morning person than Mitchie was. She normally had trouble waking up after a good night's sleep, and recently she'd hardly been getting any sleep at all. Caitlyn had been working late every night this week, so it took her even longer than usual to gain semiconsciousness.

"What time is it?" she asked in something that came out as half-sentence, half-yawn.

"Six!" Mitchie exclaimed. "In the morning!"

It took a moment for this to sink in, but when it did, Caitlyn panicked. "It's not six," she stammered, as her eyes finally focused on her clock. "It's 6:03. Do you know what that means?"

"Yeah," Mitchie said. "It means I should be asleep."

"No," Caitlyn informed her as she sat bolt upright, suddenly wide awake. "It means I'm already running three minutes late. We've got to stay on schedule today."

"No," Mitchie said sleepily as she

picked up the pillow she had thrown at Caitlyn and headed back for her own bed. "*You* have to stay on schedule. *I* have to go back to sleep."

Mitchie crawled under the covers and pulled them up over her head. It took Caitlyn all of two seconds to pull them back off.

"You can't go back to sleep!" Caitlyn said excitedly. "Today is Sound Off!"

Sound Off was the name of Camp Rock's "game" day. It was a really big deal for a lot of the campers, especially Caitlyn. Mitchie, though, was much too tired to get excited about anything—except sleeping.

"I'm curious—is one of the Sound Off games called Keep Mitchie Awake?" she asked.

"No," Caitlyn answered.

"Good." Mitchie smiled. "That means I can go back to sleep."

There was no way Caitlyn was going to let that happen. "Trust me, you don't want to miss any of it. Sound Off is a total blast. Besides, I've spent a lot of time working on it, and I could use your support. I really want the day to go well," Caitlyn said, referring to the cause of her recent streak of late nights. Brown Cesario, the director of Camp Rock, had selected her to be one of the Sound Off commissioners.

As the commish, as Brown liked to call her, Caitlyn was in charge of conceiving, planning, and designing most of the games along with her two partners—Peggy Dupree and Shane Gray. The only rule that Brown had given them was that Sound Off had to be FM/AM, which stood for "fun, musical, and messy."

"Just because I want to go back to sleep, doesn't mean I'm not looking forward to it," Mitchie said as she tried to pry the covers back out of Caitlyn's white-knuckled grip. "It's just that if I'm well rested, I can get into it more. Besides, the first event isn't until nine. I don't need three hours to get ready for a potato-sack race."

"First of all," Caitlyn replied. "It's not a potato-sack race. Any camp can have a potato-sack race. This is Camp Rock. It has to be FM/AM. We're having the Hip-Hop Hippity-Hop in a Sack Race. And, that's not even the first event. The first event is the Disco Duck Walk. No wait, we changed that last night. Now it's the Hard-Rock Rock Climb."

Mitchie stared at her friend. This was a lot to absorb so early in the morning, but she could tell there was no stopping Caitlyn. It looked like going back to sleep was definitely out of the question.

"*And*, you can't just roll out of bed and compete," Caitlyn continued. "You've got to meet with your team and figure out who's doing which events. You need to come up with a game plan. You need to eat a healthy breakfast and give it time to digest. And you should stretch properly. It's a whole day's worth of events. You don't want to start cramping up around the Reggae Row Off."

"And I don't want to fall asleep in the middle of the hippity-hop thing, either," Mitchie added.

Caitlyn took a calming breath and relaxed. "I know," she said. "I guess I'm a little excited about this."

"You don't say," Mitchie remarked with a laugh.

"It's just that I want it to go well," she admitted. "Sound Off is one of my favorite things about Camp Rock, and if it doesn't go well this year, it will be all my fault."

"Don't worry," Mitchie assured her. "It's going to be off-the-charts great. I know it!"

"You think so?" Caitlyn asked. "Because it hasn't seemed like you've been looking forward to this."

Mitchie felt a little guilty. In all honesty, she wasn't excited about Sound Off at all, but she had hoped her roommate hadn't picked up on it. "If that's the case," Mitchie said, "it's only because I won't be on a team with you. That would be way more fun."

"That is a bummer," Caitlyn agreed.

Normally they would have been on the same team because campers competed by cabin. But since Caitlyn, Peggy, and Shane were organizing the day, they weren't partaking in the actual events. Instead, Mitchie had taken Peggy's spot on the girls from Vibe Cabin's team. That meant that she was going to be on the same team as Tess Tyler.

Tess and Mitchie had been through a lot of ups and downs at Camp Rock. Originally, they had been friends, but they had had a big falling out and become sort-of enemies for a while. Now they were finding a middle ground, but a day of crazy competition might be more than their budding friendship—and Mitchie's patience—could handle.

"Besides," Caitlyn added, "Vibe Cabin

needs all the help it can get."

"What do you mean by that?" Mitchie asked.

"By what?" Caitlyn answered, suddenly coy.

"Why does Vibe Cabin need all the help it can get?"

"You know, it *is* early," Caitlyn said, completely ignoring the question. "Maybe you should go back to sleep for a little bit."

"You still haven't answered me," Mitchie pointed out. "Why does Vibe need help?"

"Didn't I tell you?" Caitlyn asked. "I totally thought I mentioned it. It's not a big deal."

"You told me that Sound Off was fun and exciting and the best day all summer," Mitchie said, mimicking Caitlyn's enthusiasm. "But you didn't say anything about Vibe Cabin needing help."

"Well," Caitlyn said, "you know how Tess

is really good at singing and dancing and pretty much everything?"

Mitchie laughed. "Yeah, I kind of noticed that."

"Well," Caitlyn said with a shrug, " 'pretty much everything' doesn't include Sound Off."

"What are you talking about?" Mitchie asked.

Caitlyn shrugged. "She's no good at sports. No good at all."

This surprised Mitchie. Tess seemed pretty athletic in dance class, and she certainly was competitive. Mitchie had just assumed she'd be a natural at sports.

"Seriously?"

"Seriously," Caitlyn confirmed. "And you know Tess doesn't like to look bad. So the whole day kind of puts her in a grumpy mood."

"Oh." Mitchie gulped.

"You might want to get over there and start warming her up," Caitlyn said. Then she looked at the clock and realized that she was falling further behind. "Now I'm *eleven* minutes behind schedule!"

Reaching down, she grabbed the giant Sound Off binder she had been carrying around all week and hurried for the door.

"Relax," Mitchie told Caitlyn as she left. "It's a daylong event. I don't want your brain cramping up by the time we reach the Reggae Row Off."

"Thanks," Caitlyn said over her shoulder. "I'll see you out there."

As she watched her friend leave, Mitchie felt a pang of guilt. Caitlyn had worked non-stop getting things ready for Sound Off, and Mitchie was kind of dreading the day's events. Like Tess, Mitchie was not good at sports. And that had always frustrated her.

If there was a beat, Mitchie could move with perfect precision. But if there was a ball, she seemed to have two left feet. She had been embarrassed on more than one

11

occasion at Camp Rock, and she was pretty sure this day would provide even more opportunities to look silly. On top of it all, she would be dealing with a grumpy and equally uncoordinated Tess.

CHAPTER TWO

In all the times that she had eaten at the Mess Hall of Fame, Mitchie had never really paid any attention to the plaques that hung on the wall near the kitchen. They were clustered under a pair of old wooden paddles which had been painted to read CAMP ROCK and SOUND OFF. There was a different plaque for every year since the beginning of camp. Each plaque featured the names of the top three cabins as well as the winners of two individual awards—the Big Enchilada and the Golden Drumstick.

Mitchie had no idea what either the Big Enchilada or the Golden Drumstick was or how it had anything to do with Sound Off, but she smiled when she saw some familiar names on the plaques. Caitlyn had won the Drumstick, and Shane had won the Big Enchilada during his last year as a camper.

"My proudest moment."

Mitchie turned to find that the pop star—and current camp counselor—Shane Gray had walked up behind her. He was wearing a striped referee's shirt and had a whistle on a string around his neck. Despite the odd apparel, he looked every inch the pop star—from his dark hair to his brooding eyes.

"What was?" she asked.

"Winning the Big Enchilada," he said

as though it had to be incredibly obvious. "As far as I'm concerned, it was right up there with the day Connect Three got our first gold record."

"What's the Big Enchilada?"

"It's the last event of Sound Off," he said with a big smile. "It's an obstacle course that runs through the whole camp. It's beyond crazy."

"And winning that is your proudest moment?" Mitchie teased. She had a hard time believing that the lead singer of one of the hottest bands in the universe could get pumped over an obstacle-course win. Still, ever since she and Shane became friends, he'd been surprising her. Today was no exception.

"Absolutely," he replied, a smile lighting up his handsome face. "At the end, I was going head-to-head with both Jason and Nate, and I *just* beat them to the finish line. It was *sweeeeet*."

Mitchie was still laughing at the image of the bandmates duking it out when Caitlyn and Peggy walked over to them. Caitlyn was in heavy-duty panic mode as she flipped through the giant binder that contained every detail about anything and everything to do with Sound Off.

"We start in twenty-seven minutes and thirteen seconds," she said as she checked her watch. "We need to make sure that we've got the stopwatches, the whistles, and the disco ball."

"Disco ball?" Mitchie repeated, perplexed.

"It's all ready," Peggy reassured Caitlyn.

"Peggy and I already went through the checklist twice," Shane added.

Caitlyn gave him a look. "The original checklist? The revised checklist? Or the amended revised checklist?"

"We did all three," Shane said, as Peggy and Mitchie tried not to laugh. "Just to be on the safe side."

"Good," Caitlyn said with a slightly relaxed breath. "Have you talked to Jason and Nate?"

"Jason and Nate are coming?" Mitchie asked with a smile. Shane's bandmates were known to drop by now and then.

Caitlyn cringed. "That's supposed to be a surprise."

"I didn't hear anything. Promise," Mitchie replied, holding a hand to her heart.

"Yes," Shane said to Caitlyn. "I talked to them a few minutes ago, and they're right on time."

Caitlyn nodded and then turned to Mitchie. "Here you go," she said, pulling out some papers from her binder and handing them to Mitchie one at a time. "This is the schedule of events. Here is a list of event descriptions, so you can figure out which member of your team should do what. Not every person has to participate in every event. And here is your team sign-up sheet. You're the captain, so you'll be in charge of it. Your team needs to be at the starting line no later than three minutes *before* an event is scheduled to begin."

"Whoa, team captain!" Mitchie cried, quickly trying to think of a way to get out of it. "Don't you think it should be one of the other girls? Maybe someone who has done this before?"

"It can't be Tess," Caitlyn explained. "I told you how she feels about Sound Off."

"What about Lorraine or Ella? Don't you think one of them would make a good captain?"

Caitlyn gave her a look. "If you don't want to be the captain, I can go find one of them. But since you're standing right here . . ."

Mitchie could tell that Caitlyn's feelings were a little hurt by her resistance. "No, it's not that I don't want to be captain," she answered. "I just want to make sure I don't step on any toes."

"Captain or no captain, Vibe Cabin is going to need all the help they can get," Peggy added.

"That's what I hear," Mitchie said, dreading the day more and more.

Suddenly Caitlyn seemed to remember something and started flipping through her binder.

"The sound system," she blurted out. "Have we checked it?"

"Last night," Shane told her.

"And then again about an hour ago," Peggy added.

"In other words, you're saying you haven't checked it recently," she said. "Maybe I should go look at it one more time. Just to be sure."

She turned quickly and headed outside.

"She's a little nervous," Mitchie said.

Shane laughed. "Just a little. We better go help her."

"Yeah," Peggy said.

"And, I guess I better go . . . captain my team."

"Good luck with that," Shane said.

Mitchie smiled. "Apparently I'll need it."

Mitchie looked through the papers as she walked over to the table where Lorraine Burgess and Ella Pador were eating breakfast. Lorraine's head was bent over her cereal bowl while Ella applied a fresh coat of lip gloss—her accessory of choice. There was no sign of Tess.

"Hey, guys," Mitchie said with a half wave as she reached the table, "ready for Sound Off?" She tried to sound enthusiastic, but it wasn't very convincing.

"Absolutely," Lorraine said. "Look what I've got." She held up a pink short-sleeved jersey with a big *V* on the chest. "I made them for all of us. They have our names on the back, and when we stand next to each other they spell out *Vibe*."

Mitchie flashed a big smile. Lorraine was

an excellent costume designer, and the shirt did look cool. Maybe this wasn't going to be so bad after all.

"That's awesome," Mitchie said. "They look great."

Lorraine smiled appreciatively. "Thank you."

"Here's the sign-up sheet," Mitchie said as she held it up. "We've got to figure out who's doing what events."

She handed the papers to them.

Ella, who, like Lorraine, was pretty excited about the day, laughed as she read through the event names. "Disco Duck Walk. Hip-Hop Hippity-Hop in a Sack Race. Some of these are new. This sounds like fun."

"You know," Mitchie said, warming up to the day, "I think you're right. It does sound fun."

"Oh," Ella said spotting something on the list. "I want to do the first event. The Hard-Rock Rock Climb."

"Me, too," Lorraine said. "Is it okay if we both sign up for it?"

"Absolutely," Mitchie said. "There'll be plenty of things for me and Tess to do. Speaking of Tess, where is she?"

"I'm not sure," Lorraine said as she put their names down on the list.

"I haven't seen her, either," Ella said as she continued to look through the list. "Here's an event for all of us—Capture the Keys to the Tour Bus."

"My personal favorite event," Brown said as he walked up to the table along with Dee La Duke, the Camp Rock musical director. "And it's not just because I'm the one who gets to hide the keys."

"Hey, Brown, Dee," Mitchie said.

"Good morning, Vibe team!" Brown said. "It seems like you're missing somebody."

"Yeah," Mitchie answered. "We were just trying to figure out where Tess was."

"Let's see. What was it last year?" Brown asked Dee.

"Doctor's note," she answered.

"Right." Brown nodded. "She tried to get out of Sound Off with a doctor's note. Of course, when I called the doctor, he had no memory of writing it."

"Don't you just hate forgetful doctors?" Dee joked.

"And the year before, I think it was the flu?" Brown added.

"Not the flu," she said correcting him. "It was Rocky Mountain spotted fever."

"That's right. You know, that might have worked," he said. "Except we're nowhere near the Rocky Mountains."

"And she didn't have a fever," Dee added.

Mitchie laughed. Caitlyn had told her that Tess hated Sound Off, but she didn't realize just how much the girl loathed it.

"Ah, here she comes," Brown said as he looked across the room.

Mitchie looked in the same direction and saw Tess enter the mess hall. At first, Mitchie couldn't figure out why Tess was moving the way she was moving. Then somebody stepped out of the way, and Mitchie got a good look at her teammate.

Tess was on crutches.

CHAPTER THREE

It was a struggle for Tess to make it across the mess hall on her crutches and still look graceful, but she managed. When she got close, the others could see that her ankle was taped up.

"I am so sorry, guys," Tess said as she reached the table. She addressed only the girls, as though Brown and Dee weren't there.

"I twisted it pretty bad in hip-hop dance

class yesterday," she explained, holding her foot up for them to see. "I was hoping it would get better overnight. But when I woke up this morning, it was worse."

"Are you going to be all right?" Lorraine asked, her green eyes filled with concern.

"Don't worry about me," Tess said. "I'm sure I'll be fine. I'm just not sure how much I'll be able to help the team today. It's a shame, because I was *really* looking forward to it."

Brown raised an eyebrow and shared a look with Dee. "Well, you better get off of that ankle and rest," he said as he pulled a chair out for her. "You wouldn't want to make it worse."

"But what about Sound Off?" she asked. "Is there some way I can still compete?"

"If you're injured, you're injured," he replied. "We can't risk you making it worse. I think you're going to have to sit this one out."

"Really?" Tess said, trying to sound disappointed and not happy.

"Really," he said.

Mitchie couldn't believe it. Brown was actually buying Tess's story. She had been in the hip-hop dance class with Tess the day before and didn't remember anything about her getting injured.

"My biggest concern is this week's jam," Brown added. "Do you think it will heal up in time for that?"

"I sure hope so," Tess offered. Then she bit her lip dramatically as though she were summoning up all of her strength. "Actually, I will make *sure* that it does. I will give it total rest between now and then, if that's what it takes."

"That's a relief," Brown said. "I'd hate for you to miss a jam."

Dee nodded knowingly before adding, "Although, she *will* have to miss Bruno and Carrie Ann."

Brown nodded. "That's a real shame. I'm sure they would have liked her."

It took a moment for this nugget of information to register with the others. The first to pick up on it was Ella. "*The* Bruno and Carrie Ann?" she blurted out.

"The judges from *Dancing with the Stars*?" added Lorraine.

"Right, they are on that show, aren't they?" Brown said, shrugging.

"I hadn't thought about it, but, yes, they are," Dee answered.

"We've always just known them as big-time choreographers and friends," Brown said.

Lorraine, who was still getting used to the star quality of a place like Camp Rock, could not believe her ears. "You mean you actually know Bruno and Carrie Ann? *Personally?*"

"We've known them forever." Brown nodded as though it were no big deal. "They called late last night because they're looking for some young dancers for a new music video they're working on."

"We were just about to announce it," Dee continued. "They'll be here first thing tomorrow morning to hold auditions."

"That's perfect," Tess said. "Wait until they see the new moves I've been working on. There's no way they won't pick me."

Without even thinking, she popped up from the chair and did an amazing double spin into a toe stop and followed it up with a moonwalk.

"Wow!" Brown said.

"I know," Tess said. "It's good. Isn't it?"

"It is good," he said. "And, apparently, so is your ankle."

As Mitchie tried to hide a smile, Tess slumped back into her chair. She had been totally caught!

There was an awkward pause that was broken by Ella. "Does that mean Bruno and Carrie Ann *aren't* coming?" she asked.

"Yep," Brown said with a smile. "And it also means that Tess is competing in Sound Off."

Tess started to say something, but realized it was pointless. She had fallen for their trap and had to suffer the consequences. So she just sat there and pouted as Brown and Dee walked away.

"Okay," Mitchie said after a long silence. "Now that the whole team is here, let's figure out who's doing what."

Mitchie tried to get the sign-up sheet filled out, but it was easier said than done. Tess hardly said a word, and her bad mood had a way of bringing the whole group down. After a few minutes, they decided to assign events as they went along through the day.

After breakfast, they went back to the Vibe Cabin to put on the jerseys that Lorraine had made for them. Actually, Lorraine, Ella, and Mitchie put on the jerseys. Tess was still pouting and only came back long enough to throw her crutches in the corner of the cabin. She didn't actually say that she wouldn't wear one of the shirts, but it was obvious she had no intention of doing so. She grunted and wandered off when the others suggested changing.

"I should have checked with all of you before making them," Lorraine said, trying to hide her hurt feelings. "If Tess is out, we probably shouldn't wear them."

"No," Mitchie told her. "I think they look great. I'm definitely wearing mine."

"So am I," added Ella.

"Thanks," Lorraine said, appreciating their support. "But there is one big problem."

Since it took all four of them to spell out *Vibe*, without Tess they were without a name.

"What are we?" Lorraine asked as she pointed to the mirror. "Team Vie?"

They all considered this for a moment, and then Mitchie had an idea. "You and Ella could change places," she suggested.

Lorraine crinkled her nose. "But that would make us Team Ive."

Mitchie smiled. "As in, '*I've* got a bad feeling about how this day is going to turn out.'" All three laughed.

"That's it," Ella said. "We're officially Team Ive."

Mitchie nodded, and Lorraine smiled in relief. Lorraine had spent a lot of time and effort on the shirts and would secretly have been pretty bummed if it hadn't worked out.

"Look at the time," Mitchie said, noticing a clock in the room. "We've got to get going. Caitlyn made it clear—this thing is going to start at nine o'clock on the dot."

As they walked from the cabin toward the outdoor stage—where Mitchie's sheet told them the day started—Mitchie tried to psych herself up. Sure, she hadn't exactly been looking *forward* to Sound Off. But after seeing how Tess's attitude affected the team, she realized she owed it to everybody to give it her best effort—no matter how silly she looked in the process.

The campers all congregated at the base of the stage. It turned out a lot of teams had matching—or at least similar—shirts.

"We're already in first place," Mitchie told Lorraine. "Because our shirts are the best!"

"No doubt," Ella added. "I even have a lip gloss that goes perfectly!"

The girls saw Tess standing toward the back of the group and went over to join her.

Tess didn't say anything about the shirts. Instead, she just asked, "When is this thing supposed to start? I don't see anyone in charge."

The stage was empty, which was surprising, because Sound Off was supposed to begin any moment.

"Trust me," Mitchie assured them. "It'll start."

She looked down at her watch, and at the

exact moment the second hand hit nine o'clock, the theme from the movie *Rocky* started blaring over the loudspeaker.

It was absolutely no surprise to her that Caitlyn had timed this out to the second. As the music played, Caitlyn, Shane, Peggy, Brown, and Dee all came jogging through the crowd as if they were characters from the movie. The five of them ran up onto the stage and pretended to shadowbox as the song ended. When it was over, Brown took center stage.

"Good morning, everybody," he called out to the crowd.

"Good morning!" the campers cried.

"Welcome to Sound Off. Normally, this is when I give my very inspirational speech about the importance of sportsmanship and about how it's not whether you win or lose, but how you play the game that really matters. And if you were lucky, I might even tell you about the game-winning goal I scored in an epic midtour soccer match that pitted U2 against Coldplay."

Caitlyn humorously cleared her throat, and Brown took the hint.

"But Caitlyn has us running on a tight schedule," he continued, "so I'll skip all that and just remind you that we only have one rule at Sound Off. It's got to be FM/AM. And what does that mean?"

"Fun, musical, and messy!" the kids cheered in unison. Most of them had heard it many times before.

"Exactly," Brown said as he stepped back. "But believe me, that goal was beautiful. Bono cried tears of joy. And if you want to hear about it, I'll be glad to tell you later at lunch or dinner. Just come find me."

Caitlyn shook her head good-naturedly as she moved up to the front of the stage.

From the crowd, Mitchie let out a big whistle to show her support.

"Welcome to Sound Off," Caitlyn said. "I

know we have some newbies in the crowd, so I'll go over the basics. There are eight events, and every cabin receives a score for each event depending on things such as how quickly you finish. At the end of the day, we give awards to the three cabins with the highest scores. We also crown a winner of the Big Enchilada, which is our one-of-a-kind, unbelievable obstacle course, and present the Golden Drumstick to the camper who shows the most spirit."

The campers all clapped and cheered.

"Now before we get started, do you want to say anything?" Caitlyn said, turning to Peggy.

Peggy started to step forward, but then changed her mind and shook her head. Peggy didn't mind singing in front of an audience, but public speaking was not her strong suit.

"Okay, then," Caitlyn said. "Now, I'd like to invite a past winner of the Big Enchilada to provide us with some music to get us in the mood. Give it up for . . . Shane Gray."

There was more applause as Shane began playing his guitar. After a few riffs, he moved up to the microphone.

"I say *Sound*, you say *Off*," he chanted. "Sound . . ."

"Off!" replied the campers, getting into it.

"I say *Sound*, you say *Off*," he sang again. "Sound . . ."

"Off!"

Shane continued playing the guitar and, in the process, turned a call-and-response sequence into a bluesy little song.

"Now I don't know, but I've been told . . ." he sang.

"I don't know but I've been told!" shouted the campers.

"Camp Rock records all go gold!"

Mitchie smiled as she and the others repeated it back to him.

"And I don't know, but it's been sung . . ." he continued.

"I don't know, but it's been sung!"

"That Camp Rock is number one!"

The campers took this and kept the chant going for a little while. After a few more times, Shane brought it all to a close.

"I think they're ready," he told Caitlyn with a nod before turning back to face the campers. "It's time to rock out at the rock wall!"

CHAPTER FOUR

Music was at the heart of everything at Camp Rock, and Brown made sure the campers were exposed to a wide variety of musical styles and techniques. He wanted them to leave well-rounded musicians. But Camp Rock was about more than music. Brown also wanted them to develop healthy habits.

That wasn't too hard when they were

surrounded by fresh air, hills, and a beautiful lake. He also spent a lot of time with Mitchie's mom—who was the camp chef—planning meals to see that everyone ate a healthy but camp-themed diet. And he insisted that the camp maintain a strong sports-and-fitness program—which explained the supercool rock-climbing wall.

The wall was about twenty feet high and had two side-by-side climbing lanes. There was a bell at the top of each lane, which normally was used for the campers to signal that they had reached the top. But for Sound Off, the bell had a more musical purpose.

When everyone got together at the wall, Caitlyn, Shane, and Peggy started stamping and clapping in time. They were imitating the opening of the Queen song "We Will Rock You." It did not take long for the others to recognize the song and join in.

"All right, everybody," Caitlyn said once

the noise had died down. "Welcome to our first event, the Hard-Rock Rock Climb. I see you all know the song, which is good."

She went on to explain how the event worked. Each team would select two players to climb up the wall at the same time. When they reached the top, they had to ring the bells in unison to the song's opening beat. Whichever team accomplished the task the fastest would win the highest number of points.

Mitchie smiled. It sounded like a cool event . . . and she wasn't going to have to do it. She liked climbing the rock wall, but she wasn't very fast. Who knew how long they'd have to wait for her to get to the top? Luckily, Lorraine and Ella both loved climbing and had both volunteered. Mitchie and Tess would need only to cheer them on from the ground.

Mitchie's teammates went toward the end. When it was their turn, Lorraine and Ella made it to the top faster than any of the other teams that had gone before them. Mitchie was really impressed, and she high-fived both girls when they got back down on the ground. Even Tess popped out of her funk long enough to congratulate them. After all, Tess *did* like winning.

Unfortunately, two other teams, including Mac Wilson and Colby Miller from the Rhythm Cabin, beat Lorraine and Ella's score, but heading into the second event, Vibe was in third place.

Unlike the Hard-Rock Rock Climb, the Disco Duck Walk was a four-person event. That meant that Mitchie and Tess would have to leave the sidelines and participate. It was a relay race, and each member of the team had to put on a pair of scuba flippers and waddle like a duck from the starting line down to the edge of the lake—called the "duck pond"—grab a rubber duck, and bring it back. The first team to bring back four rubber ducks was declared the winner.

Brown and Dee heightened the theme by playing duck calls and wearing some rather "seventies" wigs. It got people laughing— and moving.

Since she had been scuba diving a couple of times with her parents and was the only one who felt remotely comfortable in flippers, Lorraine was the first to go for the Vibe team. While the other campers struggled, she quickly moved into the lead. As her team cheered her on, Lorraine became the first one to make it to the water's edge and grab a rubber duck.

She waddled back to the starting line and quickly pulled off the flippers and handed them to Mitchie, who hurriedly started to put them on.

"Awesome job," Mitchie said as she struggled with the rubber footwear. She tried to block out all her fears and self-consciousness. After all, as she looked around, most of the others were having a hard time walking in the flippers. Looking foolish seemed to be just another part of the day. Besides, since her team was in the lead, she didn't have any people bumping into her.

"The trick is not to rush," Lorraine said. "If you rush, you'll catch your flippers and trip. Also, look out when you get close to the lake. The mud makes it pretty slippery."

Mitchie nodded and started toward the water. It was difficult, but Lorraine's tip really helped. She didn't rush, and that kept her from falling over. She wasn't as fast as Lorraine had been, but she was still in the lead when she got to the lake.

But that was only half of the race. Her foot slipped a couple of times in the mud, but she managed to get a rubber duck without falling over. As she made her way back, a couple of teams passed her. Surprisingly, Mitchie didn't panic. By that point, she had gotten a feel for the flippers and was making good time.

"Keep going, Mitchie!" Lorraine cheered.

"Yeah," Tess added, a little less enthusiastically, but Mitchie could tell the other girl was getting into it.

"Super job!" Ella cried as Mitchie arrived back at her team. She took the flippers from Mitchie and quickly headed for the lake. She was even faster than Lorraine. She not only caught up with every team that had passed them, she actually managed to build a decent lead.

"Don't rush, and watch out for the mud," Mitchie reminded Tess, as the other girl grabbed the flippers and put them on.

"Got it," Tess said, nodding. She took off in first place, and for the first few yards she was doing well.

"Come on, Tess!" her Vibe teammates shouted. "You can do it."

Meanwhile, the lead Ella had built them

was fading. Colby had caught up with Tess and was giving her a duck walk for her money. If she was frustrated, she didn't show it. She just smiled and tried her best to keep up with him.

Then she looked over her shoulder and saw that a bunch of other teams were closing in on her. Instantly, she panicked and sped up, which was the exact opposite of what Lorraine and the others had told her to do.

The faster she tried to go, the more she tripped over the ends of her flippers. By the time she reached the water's edge, most of the other teams had caught up to her. She was so focused on that, she completely forgot the other key piece of advice.

"Watch out for the mud!" Mitchie shouted from the other end.

But it was too late. Tess took a step on the muddy lake shore and instantly lost her balance. She flailed in an attempt to catch herself, but it was no use. She landed hard on her butt with a big muddy splash.

The Vibe girls cringed. But then, to their surprise, Tess struggled to her feet. Carefully, she made her way down to the water to get a rubber duck.

Unfortunately, when she reached down, she lost her balance again, and this time she fell face first—right into the water.

The onlookers started laughing good-naturedly, as most people knew that mishaps like this were all part of the fun. But the girls from Vibe knew that not everyone was laughing. When Tess stood back up, she was drenched from head to toe and the look she leveled at the spectators was so cold Mitchie was surprised the water at her feet didn't freeze. Pulling off her flippers, Tess stormed off toward the cabin, leaving her team stranded.

Most of the teams were too caught up in the race to realize how upset Tess was, but the Vibe girls knew. They exchanged worried looks.

"Someone better go talk to her," Mitchie said.

Lorraine and Ella stared at her pointedly. It took a moment for Mitchie to realize they wanted *her* to be the one.

"Why me?" Mitchie asked.

"You're the captain," Lorraine said.

Mitchie sighed. "I knew that 'captain' thing would come back to haunt me."

It looked as though she had no choice. Squaring her shoulders, Mitchie took a deep breath and headed for the cabin—and Tess.

CHAPTER FIVE

Tess might not have been into sports, but she was a pretty fast runner. At least, that was what Mitchie thought when she arrived at the cabin to find Tess already there.

Tess was still soaking wet and was angrily digging around for a towel to dry herself off. When she heard Mitchie come in, she just looked up and glared at her.

"Hey," Mitchie said sheepishly.

"What do you want?" Tess snapped.

"Well," Mitchie began, searching for the right words, "I wanted to make sure you're okay. You fell pretty hard in the mud."

"I'm fine," Tess said. "Thank you."

Mitchie didn't say anything for a moment. Instead, she pulled a fresh towel off of Ella's bunk and tossed it to Tess. She nodded her thanks and started to dry off her hair.

"I also wanted to see if you were going to be coming back to Sound Off," Mitchie continued. "I know you're not a big fan. But we need four people for some of the events. We need you."

Tess continued to angrily rub her hair. Then she suddenly stopped. "Why do we even have to do this?" she asked, looking over at Mitchie. "What purpose does it serve?"

"I don't know," Mitchie answered honestly. "Because it's fun, I guess."

"Yeah. Total humiliation," Tess said. "That's loads of fun."

"Good point," Mitchie said, laughing. "But you shouldn't feel humiliated."

Tess shot her a look. "Did you see me out there?"

"Yeah, I did." Mitchie said, nodding. "You were pretty bad."

"Gee, thanks," Tess replied. "Don't sugarcoat it on my behalf."

"But so what?" Mitchie went on, ignoring Tess's sarcasm. "So you're not good at running in flippers. You're an incredible singer and dancer. I think if you asked most people here, that's what they'd rather be good at."

"That's a good point," Tess replied.

"It's not like I was doing much better," Mitchie went on. "I just managed to stay out of the lake."

"Smart choice," Tess joked. "By the way, you're a really good singer and dancer, too."

Mitchie smiled. Tess was not one to throw around compliments. She must have meant it. Maybe this game day would be good for more than just a plaque. Maybe she and Tess would finally put their past behind them.

"I'm certainly *not* good at sports," Mitchie said. "In gym class, I'm always the last one picked."

Tess laughed. "So am I. And, of course, my mother is an amazing athlete. Last year she ran the New York City Marathon with Diddy."

Mitchie cringed. "I think I saw that on Hot Tunes."

"Oh, yeah," Tess said. "They had cameras following their every move."

"And I thought the trophy case was bad," Mitchie said.

"What trophy case?"

Mitchie rolled her eyes. "The trophy case at my school. My mom was some star basketball player, and there's a picture of her in the case next to the gym."

"And you've got to pass it every day at school?"

Mitchie nodded.

"Brutal," Tess said. "It's just like those plaques up in the mess hall."

"Yeah. I was looking at those today," Mitchie said, nodding.

"My first summer, I was determined to get my name up there," Tess said. "That was before I realized how uncoordinated I was. And here's the part I don't get. *Why* am I uncoordinated? It's not like any of these events are harder than those dance moves I've been working on."

"You mean the one you 'sprained your ankle' on?" Mitchie joked, making air quotes with her fingers.

Tess laughed. "Yeah, that one."

"Show it to me again," Mitchie said.

Tess did the move. It was a spin that led into a toe stop and ended with a moonwalk.

"That really is cool," Mitchie said.

"But if I can do that, why can't I do a silly duck walk?" Tess wanted to know. "What's the trick I'm not getting?"

"I think it's the music," Mitchie observed.

"What do you mean?" Tess asked, her blue eyes curious.

"Well, when you dance, you hear music," Mitchie explained. "The music is what helps make your body move so well. And when you're doing sports, there's no music."

Tess cocked her head as she absorbed Mitchie's observation. "You know, you might be right."

They both smiled. It occurred to Mitchie that this was the first time that she and Tess had ever really just talked—like friends. It was funny. Of all the things they could bond over, it *would* be something neither one was any good at.

While Mitchie and Tess were bonding, Caitlyn was stressing—big-time. After two events, Sound Off was already falling behind her meticulously orchestrated schedule.

The drama of Tess falling in the water and

Mitchie chasing after her was bad enough. After all, that meant half of the Vibe team was gone and not ready for the next event. But Caitlyn didn't even have time to worry about that, because she had a bigger problem on her hands.

She wasn't ready, either.

Jason and Nate were supposed to have arrived at Camp Rock thirty minutes earlier. There was still no sign of them—and they were part of the next event.

Now she was standing with Brown, Dee, Peggy, and Shane, her heart racing and her palms sweaty. Meanwhile, Shane was trying to reach the guys on his cell phone.

"Any luck?" Caitlyn asked hopefully.

Shane just shook his head. "There's no service."

Caitlyn took a deep breath and started flipping through her binder. She had no choice. She'd just have to find another event and swap the order.

"We could do the Connect Three-Legged Race," she offered.

Brown gave her a look.

"Except, not without Connect Three," she continued as she resumed flipping. "How about the Hip-Hop Sack Race or the Reggae Row Off?"

Suddenly, there was a loud rumbling from the camp's entrance. Everyone turned.

"There they are," Peggy said happily. The Connect Three bus was pulling into the parking lot. The side was painted with the cover art from the band's soon-to-be-released new album. From the front of the bus, Jason pulled a cord, and the horn blared a musical tune that caught everyone's attention.

It was like a rock-and-roll ice-cream truck. Within moments, it was surrounded by campers.

"Hello, Camp Rock," Jason said as he stepped off the bus. He looked down and saw an anxious Caitlyn making her way to the front of the group. "And hello, Caitlyn."

"Tell me you remembered," she said to him.

"Remembered what?" he said, teasing her. "The Jell-O balloons? Of course we did."

"Awesome." Caitlyn checked her watch. They were a little behind schedule, but they could make it up.

Jason went back into the bus, and when he came out of he was carrying a large cooler. Nate was right behind him with a second one.

"Here is the Jell-O," Jason said, opening the lids of the two coolers. "And here are the balloons." He unzipped his backpack and pulled out a brand-new bag of balloons.

He smiled, but he could tell by Caitlyn's wide-eyed stare that something was wrong. He looked down at the bowls of Jell-O that filled both coolers and then looked at the balloons. Finally it dawned on him.

"Wait a second," he said. "Was the Jell-O

supposed to be *in* the balloons?"

Caitlyn started hyperventilating.

"Uncle Brown," Shane said; he was calling for help.

"I'm on it," Brown said as he moved in and put a reassuring hand on Caitlyn's shoulder. "Hey, sweetie, why don't you take a break for a minute? And Peggy, why don't you and Dee go up to the kitchen and see if Mrs. Torres can help you figure out a way to get all of that Jell-O into those balloons?"

"We can use cake icers," Dee said. "I think we've got two of them in the kitchen."

"Perfect," Brown said. "Shane, what do you say we get everything ready for the Connect Three-Legged Race?"

"Sure," Shane said.

All throughout this exchange, Caitlyn stood in a motionless daze, staring at the coolers filled with Jell-O. Finally, she spoke, answering a question from earlier.

"Yes," she said, in disbelief. "The Jell-O

needs to be *in* the balloons. That's why they're called Jell-O balloons!"

Brown gave her another reassuring pat on the shoulder. "I think they've finally figured that out. Why don't you go up to the kitchen and help them?"

CHAPTER SIX

When Mitchie rejoined her group, she was alone. She and Tess had had a good talk, but at the end of it, Tess hadn't said whether she was done for the day or not.

Mitchie knew the balloon toss had been scheduled to take place next. She had figured that it would still be going on, but now there was no sign of it. That meant either that her talk had gone on longer than she realized or that something had come along to upset Caitlyn's schedule.

Looking around, she tried to spot Caitlyn. Instead of her friend, she saw Brown talking to Shane and the boys from Connect Three. Whatever they were doing, they seemed to be making it up on the spot.

"How'd it go?" Ella asked as Mitchie walked up to her and Lorraine.

"Pretty good," Mitchie said. "But I don't know if we're going to see her again."

"That's kind of what we figured," Lorraine said.

"What did I miss?" Mitchie asked.

"A lot, actually," Ella said. "Apparently, Jason and Nate were supposed to bring a whole bunch of Jell-O–filled balloons. Except, they didn't realize the Jell-O was supposed to go *inside* the balloons. So there have been some schedule changes."

Mitchie groaned. "I don't imagine Caitlyn took that well."

"Not really," Ella said. "She went up to the kitchen with Peggy and Dee to try to fix the balloons."

Mitchie knew how hard Caitlyn had worked. She hoped this wasn't making her too crazy.

"So instead of the Rhythm and Balloons, we're going to have the Connect Three-Legged Race," Lorraine added as she handed her the sign-up sheet.

"Okay," Mitchie said, looking it over. "That takes three of us." There weren't a lot of options, so she started to write in the names: Mitchie, Ella, and—she looked up and something made her smile—"Tess?"

The others turned to see that Tess had come back to join them. She was wearing her pink Vibe shirt.

"Did I miss anything?" she asked.

"Nothing," Ella said.

"Nice shirt," Mitchie commented.

"My other one's wet," Tess said. She looked

at Lorraine and added, "Besides, this one's too nice not to wear."

Lorraine smiled, and for the first time all day, the group felt like a real team.

"You ready to make a fool of yourself?" Mitchie asked.

Tess smiled and nodded. "I wouldn't be here if I wasn't."

"Great," Mitchie said. "Then let's do this— together."

They gathered with the other teams and watched carefully as Shane, Nate, and Jason demonstrated the proper technique for doing the Connect Three-Legged Race. Unfortunately for everyone, Jason was the one doing the explaining. He had a way of . . . complicating things.

"Don't think of it as a *Connect* . . . three-legged race," he told them. "Think of it as a Connect Three . . . legged race. Do you understand the difference?"

The campers stared at him blankly.

"Why don't you let me try," Shane said, much to everyone's relief.

"This was something we came up with back when we were at Camp Rock," he began. "Instead of a normal three-legged race, which has two people tied together, this one actually uses three people."

He demonstrated by standing between Nate and Jason and putting his arms around their shoulders so that the three of them were linked together.

Brown bent over and quickly tied one of Shane's legs to Jason's and the other to Nate's.

"You see," Jason said, trying to jump back into the explanation, "Brown has connected *three* of us, so it's Connect Three."

"I think they get it," Nate said. "Why don't we show them how to walk?"

"Good idea!" Shane added. "It takes a little getting used to, so you should practice before the race begins."

"This can't go well," Mitchie said as she took the middle position. Tess was to her right and Ella to her left, and she had her arms around both of them. Lorraine tied their ankles together, making sure the bands were strong enough to hold, but not too tight.

The trio took a couple of practice steps— and promptly fell.

"Think dance class," Mitchie joked.

Tess's eyes lit up. "You're right. That's exactly what we should do."

Ella looked confused. "We should what?" she asked.

"We should act like this is dance class," Tess explained. "We choose a song and sing it as we race. It will give us rhythm."

"That's brilliant!" Mitchie said, getting it. "If we move on the beat, we'll keep in step perfectly. Just like when we're in dance class."

Ella started nodding. "Okay, but what song should we pick?"

Unfortunately, the race was about to begin. They didn't have much time.

"On your marks," Brown announced.

This only made them flustered. "What about one of your mother's songs?" Mitchie suggested.

"Which one?"

"How about 'Bound by Love'?" Mitchie offered.

Tess shook her head. "It's too slow. We'd finish dead last."

"Get set," Brown announced.

Ella just blurted out the first song title she could think of. "How about 'Jingle Bells'?"

"Go!" Brown shouted.

Every team took off except for the three girls from the Vibe Cabin. After a moment they all shared a look.

"'Jingle Bells'!" they cried in unison, and they began singing.

As strange as it was for the three of them to be singing about sleigh rides and snow in the middle of summer, it was even stranger to see that their plan was working. They were rocking. Or at least caroling.

While the other teams struggled to keep in step, the Vibe team just sang "Jingle Bells" and rapidly moved through the crowd. Near the halfway point, they moved into first place. Back at the starting line, Lorraine was furiously cheering them on.

Not only was the song helping them all keep in step, it was also distracting the other teams, who couldn't quite figure out what the girls were doing.

The only problem came when they ran out of lyrics, about five yards short of the finish line. They stumbled a bit, but still finished well ahead of everyone else. Only when they were at the end did they collapse.

The first person to congratulate them at the finish line was Brown. After they untied their ankles, he helped them up and gave each one a high five. The last one up was

Tess. "I'm glad your ankle's feeling better," he said with a wink.

"So am I," she replied, a huge smile on her face.

The team spirit that had worked so well in the Connect Three-Legged Race carried over into the next event, the much-delayed balloon toss.

Caitlyn and the others returned from the kitchen with coolers filled with Jell-O Balloons. And now the Jell-O was *inside* the balloons—where it was supposed to be.

Caitlyn was pretty stressed by the whole situation, but she did flash a big smile when she looked up at the scoreboard and saw that the Vibe team had won the last event.

"How did that happen?" she asked Mitchie when she caught up to her friend.

Mitchie shrugged. "Just lucky, I guess."

"Luck had nothing to do with it," Lorraine said firmly. "You should have seen the three of them. They were amazing!"

Unfortunately, while the team spirit carried over from one event to the next, the results weren't the same. The object of the Rhythm and Balloons Toss was for teammates to spread apart and toss balloons to each other—to the beat of a popular song. If two teammates succeeded in catching the balloon without its bursting open, they moved farther apart and tried again.

Mitchie paired up with Lorraine, but this time they were one of the first teams to be eliminated. When Mitchie tried to catch the balloon above her head, it burst open, covering her with giant globs of raspberry Jell-O.

Tess and Ella lasted a couple of rounds longer but were knocked out when Tess misjudged a balloon and it landed right on top of her. Jell-O filled her hair and began to drip down into her shirt. The others took a deep breath as they waited for her to explode in anger, but they were in for a pleasant surprise. She just laughed as she tried to shake off the Jell-O.

After four events, the Vibe team was having a great time. And much to their surprise, they were still doing pretty well in the competition. Placing third in the rock climb and first in the three-legged race had left them tied for fifth with just one more event left before lunch.

CHAPTER SEVEN

All the campers got together in front of the stage for the next competition. Although none of the girls from Mitchie's team were saying it out loud, the fact that they were in fifth place was foremost in their thoughts. Suddenly, their being one of the three teams on the plaque was a real possibility.

"We have one more event before we break for lunch," Brown said, "and it's my favorite one. Other camps play capture the flag, which is cool. But here at Camp Rock, we play a game called Capture the Keys to the Tour Bus."

Everybody laughed.

"It is a game that was inspired by a time when yours truly misplaced the keys to our bus while my band was on tour. Our manager gave me thirty minutes to find them before he was going to rent another bus and make me pay for it out of my own pocket. Luckily, my mates pitched in and we found those keys with three minutes to spare.

"Now you've got the same deal," he went on. "I've hidden the keys to the Connect Three bus somewhere here at Camp Rock. If you find the keys, go to the bus and blast the horn. If you do it in less than thirty minutes, not only do you win the race, you also get to have a rock-star lunch in the bus with the band."

This bit of information led to cheers and applause.

"We're even going to give you a clue," Brown added with a twinkle in his eyes.

Shane walked out with an electric guitar, and the campers went wild again.

Lorraine stifled a squeal. Even though she had been at Camp Rock for a while now, she still couldn't get over the fact that they were privy to little concerts from *the* Shane Gray.

"Shane here is going to play a little something for you," Brown said with a smile. "You've got to pay close attention, because it's the only clue you're going to get."

Shane smiled and played four notes on the guitar.

Now Mitchie was really confused. "That's it?"

"What's the clue?" Lorraine asked, somewhat disappointed there had been no lyrics or signature dance moves.

Tess just shrugged.

Brown was delighting in the difficulty every one was having. "I told you to pay close attention," he said. "All right, Shane, play it for them one more time."

Shane nodded, got back into a serious rock-star pose—and played the same four notes.

Brown held up a stopwatch. "That's it. No more help. You have thirty minutes."

The teams didn't need any more encouragement. Immediately, they ran off in every direction. They would turn the camp upside down if it meant finding those keys.

The Vibe team, however, stayed where they were. They weren't just going to run around like chickens with their heads cut off. They wanted to come up with a plan.

"So the music is the clue. Any ideas?" Mitchie asked.

The girls pondered silently. "Did it sound like the beginning of a song?" Ella finally asked.

"That could be it," Lorraine said. "Maybe the title of the song is the clue."

Tess hummed it out loud. "It sounds a

little familiar," she said, "but I can't quite place it."

She hummed the notes again, and this time something about them caught her attention. "You know, they sound a little bit like the opening to that David Cook song."

She sang the first notes of the song, and the others joined in. "I think you're right," Ella said.

"What if the clue isn't the name of the song?" Lorraine asked. "What if it's the name of the singer: *Cook*."

They all shared a look and smiled. "The kitchen."

They tried to keep their excitement down. The other teams were running around in every direction, and the girls didn't want to attract too much attention as they headed toward the kitchen.

Slyly keeping an eye out for the others, they began walking toward the mess hall. Unfortunately, they noticed two of the guys from Rhythm Cabin, Colby and Mac, were headed in the same direction.

"Check it out," Lorraine said, nodding toward them.

"Think they figured it out?" Ella asked.

As if in response, having just noticed the girls, the boys started sprinting toward the kitchen. The girls chased after them, resulting in a simultaneous dash to the mess hall.

"Look in the cupboard!" Mitchie told Ella as they burst through the door. "I'll check the pantry."

Within moments, the kitchen was a whirlwind. While Tess and Lorraine were crawling around on their hands and knees looking under everything, Colby sifted through a bag of flour and Mac searched in the refrigerator.

When Connie Torres walked into her kitchen, she was stunned. "Everybody, stop!" she shouted, raising her voice not so much in anger as to be heard over all the noise. "What is going on here?"

"We're looking for the tour-bus keys!" Mitchie blurted out.

"There are no keys in what *was* my very clean kitchen," Connie said.

"Are you sure?" Colby asked. "Because we're pretty sure it was that one David Cook song. And *Cook* led us here."

"That's what we thought," Tess said.

Having heard Connie's yell, Brown came rushing into the room.

"Okay," he said, as he scanned the flour-covered kitchen. "Next time I should announce that the kitchen is off limits. Sorry about that, Connie."

"That would be a good idea," Connie said, nodding.

Tess slumped. "You mean the keys are *not* in here?"

"No!" Brown exclaimed. "They're not."

Without missing a beat, the boys from

Rhythm Cabin bolted outside and started searching again. Mitchie, though, felt bad and started to clean up. The rest of the girls from her team joined in to help.

"Don't worry about it," Mitchie's mom said when her shock wore off. "You're in the middle of a competition. We can fix this later."

They didn't need to be told twice. "Thanks, Mom," Mitchie said. Turning to her team, she gestured for them to follow her.

The four girls walked into the dining room to think about the clue some more. Once again they tried to hum it out to see if the notes could mean something else. But they couldn't quite get it.

"I need the piano," Mitchie said as she moved over to the instrument on the other side of the room. "I think it went like this."

She played four notes. First she tried them slow. Then she tried them fast. But they didn't register with anybody.

"Are you sure those are the notes?" Ella asked.

"Pretty sure," Mitchie said. "The first note was C. Then B. Then G and E." She played the notes as she said them.

Tess shook her head. "I don't think the second note was a B. I think it was an A."

Mitchie tried it and nodded. "You're right. It was an A."

"Play that a couple times," Lorraine said.

Mitchie played it through a few more times at different speeds.

"Stop!" Tess said as she smiled. "I know where the keys are."

"You do?" Mitchie said.

Tess nodded. "Let me sit down."

Mitchie got up from the piano bench, and Tess sat down. She played the four notes. "It's not a song," Tess said. "It's a word."

She played them again. Only, this time, she said the name of each note as she played it. "C.A.G.E. Cage."

79

"That is so cool!" Mitchie said. "It's hidden in a cage!" Then she paused. "Wait. *What* cage?"

Lorraine and Ella both spoke at the same time. "Rockin' Robin!"

Mitchie's eyes grew wide. That had to be it! One of the decorations that Brown had put up in B-Note—the camp's hangout and snack bar—was a stuffed bird that played the song "Rockin' Robin" if you pressed a button. The bird was in a big plastic cage.

In order to keep from attracting attention, most of the girls went in the wrong direction, acting as if they were looking for the keys in one of the rehearsal rooms. Tess, meanwhile, slipped unseen into B-Note and found the keys hidden in the bottom of Rockin' Robin's cage.

Just as the thirty minutes were about to expire, Tess hurried up to the tour bus, unlocked the door, and sounded the horn.

In a matter of seconds, the other campers surrounded the bus, amazed to see Tess standing inside it alone.

CHAPTER EIGHT

Because they had won the Capture the Tour Bus Keys event, the girls from the Vibe team were treated to a rock-star lunch on the bus along with the guys from Connect Three. The food was the same as the food that the other campers were having in the mess hall, but the surroundings made all the difference.

"I cannot believe how cool this bus is," Mitchie said as she took a bite of her grilled-cheese sandwich. "It's like a real house with wheels."

"Yeah," Ella added, looking at all of the fancy gadgets and electronics. "A totally nice and blinged-out house."

Ella wasn't joking. The bus was fully loaded with comfy couches, flat-screen televisions, video-game consoles, and a rockin' sound system that was currently playing a Justin Timberlake dance tune.

"And to think," Mitchie said, soaking it all in, "we wouldn't be here if Tess hadn't been a total genius and solved that clue."

"Let's hear it for Tess," Lorraine said raising her cup of lemonade for a toast.

"Tess!" the others responded.

Normally, Tess would have been basking in the glow of this sort of attention. But, she hadn't even heard a word of it. She was busy studying the list of remaining events and doing some quick math on a scrap of paper.

"What's that about?" Mitchie asked, pointing to the paper.

Tess looked up and smiled. "We may get on the plaque."

"What are you talking about?" Lorraine asked. She was sitting in a massage chair, so her voice vibrated as she talked.

"*The* plaque," Tess explained. "The top three teams get their names engraved on the plaque that hangs in the Music Mess Hall of Fame."

"So does the winner of the Big Enchilada," Shane added with a smile. "And I got my name on it as proof."

Nate shook his head. "I can't believe you brought that up," he said. "You did *not* deserve to win that. If I hadn't slipped on that pile of wet leaves, I would have beaten you."

"Yeah," Jason added. "And if I had been . . . faster and finished before you, I would have beaten you, too."

"Those are pretty big ifs, fellas," Shane said gleefully.

83

The boys continued giving each other a hard time, but Mitchie was focused on what Tess had just said.

"You really think so?" Mitchie asked her. "You think we could make it into the top three?"

"We've got a great chance," Tess said, "if I did all the calculations correctly."

The two of them exchanged smiles. After years of nothing but frustration when it came to sports, the chance to actually do well in a competition was almost more than they could have hoped for.

Mitchie went and sat down next to Tess. "What events are left?"

The two of them looked over the list and started plotting out their strategy.

Unlike Mitchie and her team, Caitlyn was having a lunch that was anything but fun and exciting. She barely paid attention to her sandwich as she stared at the papers spread across the table in front of her and continued to flip through her giant binder.

Brown approached and sat down next to her. "What's the matter, Commish?"

"Everything," Caitlyn said, frustrated. "The balloons were just the tip of the iceberg. We're behind schedule. We've had to rearrange the event order. I'm not sure we have everything ready for the Big Enchilada."

"Slow down," Brown said gently. "I think you're losing sight of something."

"There's something else?" she asked, panicked as she looked at her papers to see what she might have missed. "What is it?"

"It's not in those papers," he told her. "Come here a second."

Brown stood and signaled for her to follow him. Reluctantly, she got up.

"I want you to look at this." He walked her over to where the Sound Off plaques hung on the wall. "Who has won the Golden Drumstick more times than anyone else?"

"I have," Caitlyn said.

"That's not luck," Brown told her. "The Golden Drumstick is given to the camper with the most spirit. And for quite a few years, that has been you. You've won it because you've gotten into Sound Off more than any camper ever. Why?"

"Because it's so much fun."

"That's right," he said with a smile. "But you haven't looked like you've had much fun today."

"This year, I've got responsibility," she replied. "I'm supposed to make sure every-one *else* has fun."

Brown laughed. "And they are. But there's no reason you shouldn't have fun, too."

He looked at Caitlyn hopefully, but it was clear his words hadn't hit a chord—yet.

It was time to try a different tactic. "Some day you want to be a music producer, right?"

Caitlyn smiled. "Absolutely."

"And when that day comes, you're still

going to enjoy the music, aren't you?"

"Of course," she replied.

"Believe me," Brown said, pointing at the papers on the desk, "this is nothing compared to how far you'll fall behind schedule when you're trying to organize a rock-and-roll band during a recording session."

"I guess that's true," she said, her tension easing slightly.

"And it's good that it's true," he told her. "Because it's during the unplanned moments that the real musical greatness occurs. Have you ever heard of Sam Phillips?"

"Sounds familiar," she said. "He was a producer, right?"

"He wasn't *a* producer," Brown said. "He was *the* producer. He ran Sun Records, and he practically invented rock and roll. Like any good producer, he was always on the lookout for something new. Well, one day, he was auditioning a singer in his studio, and it was not going well. And it was certainly not going according to his plan. They were falling behind schedule. The studio musicians didn't think the singer was any good. The audio engineer didn't think he was any good. And Sam wasn't sure, either."

"What happened?" Caitlyn asked.

"During a break, the singer started goofing around with the microphone," said Brown. "The song he sang wasn't on the playlist they had arranged. And he sang it in a way that was very different than the way everyone else had wanted him to sing. He just sang it in his own style.

"And Sam, being a great producer, knew that he had lucked into something great," Brown continued. "He cancelled lunch, quickly got everyone back into position, and told them to start recording. Then he told the singer to do it the way he had when he was joking around. And that's how they recorded the song."

"What was the song?"

"'That's All Right, Mama,'" Brown answered.

Caitlyn didn't recognize the name. "Was it a hit?"

"You might say that," Brown said. "And so was the singer."

"Who was he?"

"Elvis Presley."

"That's cool," Caitlyn said, smiling. Then she frowned. "But what does it have to do with Sound Off?"

"It's important to plan things out, Caitlyn," Brown said with a smile. "But sometimes things don't follow the plan. There's nothing wrong with that. Everyone is having a great time—even Tess, and we know how much she hates Sound Off. You're doing a great job. So you should stop worrying about everything and enjoy it."

Caitlyn looked up at him and smiled.

"Thanks, Brown. Thanks a lot."

He just smiled, did his best Elvis pose, and began to sing as he walked away.

CHAPTER NINE

After lunch, Sound Off quickly got under way again. This time, there were some notable attitude adjustments. Brown's talk had done a world of good for Caitlyn. She was trying to remember to have a little more fun and a little less stress. She still carried her giant binder around with her, but she was determined to make an effort to enjoy herself.

Meanwhile, the girls from the Vibe team had set their sights on a top-three finish. They figured if they did well in the two remaining events, they would have an excellent chance at earning a spot on the plaque and immortality in the mess hall. After checking their math, they even realized that they had an outside shot at finishing in first place. They would have to do well in both events, but they had a chance to catch the Rhythm team, which was currently in first place.

For two girls who had been dreading Sound Off that morning, Mitchie and Tess were downright cheerful as they walked back to the stage.

"How you doing, roomie?" Mitchie asked when they reached Caitlyn.

"Going a little crazy, but I'm doing all right," she answered.

"You were right, by the way," Mitchie said.

Caitlyn gave her a confused look. "I was? About what?"

"Sound Off," Mitchie replied. "It is beyond fun."

"You've done a really great job," added Tess.

It took all Caitlyn's strength to keep her mouth from dropping open. She had been worried people wouldn't like the day, but she never even considered Tess's opinion. She had just assumed Tess would *never* like it. And here she was complimenting her! "Thanks," Caitlyn finally said, snapping out of it. "Good luck in the last few events. It looks like you guys have a shot at the plaque."

"Hard to believe, isn't it?" Mitchie said, smiling.

Caitlyn just shook her head. "Not at all."

Leaving the others to join their team, Caitlyn went up toward the stage. It was time to get ready for the next event—the Hip-Hop Hippity-Hop in a Sack Race.

It was a relay race—with a twist: all the "hopping" had to incorporate some "hipping." In other words, rhythm. The girls of Vibe needed to come up with the right strategy. They each took a couple of turns hopping inside the sack to get the feel of it.

"You should go first, Lorraine," Tess said as she watched her roommate go. "You're really fast, and we could use an early lead."

"I'll go second," Mitchie said. "I'm probably the worst jumper, so we should get me out of the way."

"Same with me for third," Tess said. "That way we can save Ella for the final leg. She can make up whatever distance Mitchie and I lose."

Everyone laughed, and Mitchie was struck by how easygoing things had become with them. They really had become a team. Tess, who normally wouldn't have admitted any weakness, was now openly joking about being bad at something.

Soon it was time. They were assigned to the outside lane of the race, right next to the Rhythm team.

"They're the ones in first," Tess whispered to her team. She nodded at the boys. "That's who we're chasing. Keep your eyes on the prize."

Shane blew his whistle, and all the teams started hopping. Just as they had hoped, Lorraine gave the team an excellent start. She moved right out in front and stayed there until the end of her turn.

When Lorraine came back across the line, she jumped right out of her sack in one fluid motion. Mitchie slid right in and started hopping. A lot of the other teams were struggling with the trade-off, which gave the Vibe team an advantage.

Mitchie wasn't nearly as fast as Lorraine, but she managed to do the whole lap without falling—a major accomplishment in her mind. A couple of teams, including Rhythm, passed her, but she knew there was plenty more race to run—or hop.

All the girls cheered wildly as Tess hopped her way through the third leg of the race. It was a real struggle, but she didn't give up the way she had during the Disco Duck Walk. She kept hopping, and when she got back to the line, her team was still in the middle of the pack, with a chance to finish in the lead.

The Rhythm team had been ahead, but Colby was having trouble getting out of his sack for the last switch. His shoe kept getting caught, and by the time Mac, their final person, started out, they were close to being in last place.

Ella closed it out for the Vibe team. Years of dance class had given her strong legs. And her three older brothers had made her very competitive. She quickly caught up with the leaders at the halfway point. As they raced to the finish, there were three teams ahead of her, but she was making up distance.

"Jump, Ella! Jump, Ella! Jump, jump, jump, Ella!" the Vibe girls cheered.

Ella made a flurry of fast jumps at the end and wound up crossing the finish line in midair. The four teams were so close that no one could tell for sure who had finished where. All eyes turned to Shane, who, as referee, had final say.

Without hesitation he called the finishing order: "First place: Tempo; second: Vibe; third: Bass Line; and fourth: Allegro."

The girls from Vibe were ecstatic. Those last furious leaps had secured them a second-place finish and moved them into third place overall. There was only one event left. If they could just keep their current position, that plaque wouldn't just be a dream.

All the campers moved down to the lake for the final team event. Every year, Sound Off ended with the Big Enchilada, but that was an individual event. The team competition came down to the Reggae Row Off. While, technically, one paddles a canoe and rows a boat, "Reggae Paddle Off" didn't sound right, so the inaccurate name had stuck.

During the summer, Mitchie had spent a lot of time paddling around the lake in canoes with Shane. But they had never been in a hurry. They had talked about life, music, and all sorts of things. Racing had never been on the agenda.

Now she would have to paddle as fast—and as straight—as she possibly could. Since there weren't enough canoes for all the teams to race in at once, it was a timed event. And as canoes only hold two passengers, each team had to pick their strongest links. For some reason, the Vibe team decided to go with Mitchie and Tess.

"Got any pointers?" Mitchie asked Shane while they put on life jackets.

"The trick is making sure both your

paddles hit the water at the same time," he explained. "That's crucial. It's what makes the canoe stay straight and go fast."

"Both at once? That's a good tip," Mitchie said appreciatively. "Thanks."

The team names were drawn from a hat to determine the order. The Vibe team went last, which was a huge advantage, because that way they'd know how all of the other teams did.

Tess had a very nice waterproof watch that she had gotten on a trip to the Caribbean with her mother. Once they knew all the other teams' times, she set two alarms using the stopwatch feature.

"If Mitchie and I finish before it goes off the first time," she explained to the rest of Team Vibe, "that means we win the whole thing."

The others smiled broadly at this and traded high fives.

"If the first one goes off, but we finish

before the second one," she added, "that means we're still in the top three and get a spot on the plaque."

What she didn't say—but what they all knew—was that if they finished after the second alarm rang, they wouldn't be on the plaque at all.

Mitchie sat in the front seat of the canoe and turned around to face her teammate. "Think fast!" she told her.

"Let's go, Vibe," Lorraine added from her spot on the shore. Standing next to her, Ella let out a cheer.

Shane stood at the end of the dock that marked the finish line. He had a green flag that he waved in the air.

"Ready?" he called out.

"Ready!" the two girls shouted in return.

"On your marks, get set, go!" He waved the flag, and the Vibe team started paddling.

Not only did they start well, but they got huge laughs from the crowd because, as they paddled, they sang "Jingle Bells." Just as they had done in the three-legged race, they were using the song to help keep them on the same beat.

But this time it wasn't helping.

No matter how hard they tried, the girls could not seem to keep in time with each other. This caused the canoe to veer off course, and they lost precious time. The harder they tried to paddle and catch up, the more off track they got.

They were about halfway through the race when the first alarm rang from Tess's watch.

"Don't slow down," Tess said. "We can still make it!"

They paddled and paddled, but continued to veer badly off course. They were getting tired and frustrated.

The second alarm went off.

They were officially exhausted. Pulling their paddles out of the water, Mitchie and

Tess struggled to catch their breath. It looked as if they were through. The plaque was no longer a possibility.

But Tess wasn't about to give up.

"We can do this!" she said from the back of the canoe. "We can't win, but we can finish this race!"

Something about the way she was cheering Mitchie on caught the attention of the other campers back on the shore. This was a side of Tess that they had never seen. Soon, everybody was rooting for them, and the most natural way to do that was for all of the campers to sing "Jingle Bells" at the tops of their lungs.

So, as a loud and thunderous chorus of "Jingle Bells" came over the lake, the girls dug in and paddled on to the finish.

CHAPTER TEN

Sound Off was almost over. But there was one final event—the Big Enchilada. The campers gathered together in front of the stage, where Brown, Dee, and Caitlyn were standing. But before this final event, Brown had a couple of announcements he wanted to make.

"I want to congratulate the Rhythm team for winning the championship," he said. "You did great today and really deserve it."

The boys from Rhythm Cabin raised their fists in celebration and Mac did a little victory dance as the other campers gave them all a big round of applause.

"And while we're at it," Brown continued, "I want to congratulate all of you. Just because your name is not on a plaque doesn't mean you aren't a winner." As he said this, he looked right at Mitchie and Tess, who both smiled and nodded back at him.

There was more applause.

"Now it's time for the Big Enchilada!" he said to loud cheers. "Can you handle it?"

"Yes!" everyone cheered in unison.

"Before we start, I want Caitlyn to give me that big binder she's been carrying all day."

Caitlyn didn't know what was going on, but she came over and handed him the binder anyway.

"You guys have all seen this today. In it, Caitlyn, Peggy, and Shane planned out every single detail of the day. They made sure that everything came together and worked perfectly. And they all deserve a huge round of applause."

There were more cheers from the other campers.

"But I've got bad news," he continued. "We're making some last-minute changes to the Big Enchilada."

He laughed and tossed the binder over his shoulder. Caitlyn looked as though she were going to pass out when she saw it hit the stage. She started to go to pick it up, but he stopped her.

"You are hereby relieved of your duties as the commissioner," he continued.

"Why?" she asked worriedly.

Brown smiled. "Because I want you and Shane and Peggy to participate in the Big Enchilada. It is the most fun race of the day, and I'd hate for you guys to miss it."

"Really?" Caitlyn asked, her eyes wide.

"If you think you can handle it," Brown said with a wink.

Caitlyn smiled. "Oh, I can definitely handle it," she assured him. She was thrilled. While she had had fun planning the events, all day long she felt as if she were missing out on the fun of competing. Now she would have her chance.

Brown went on to explain the rules of the race. The Big Enchilada was a giant obstacle course that went all around the camp. Everyone competed as an individual, and along the way there were six different tasks that had to be completed. Each task was related to something from the history of rock and roll. The finish line was at the end of the dock, and the winner was the first person to jump off the dock and into the water.

At the starting line, Caitlyn took her place alongside Mitchie and Tess.

"You've got no chance against us," Mitchie joked.

"Yeah," Tess added with a laugh. "We are all about the Big Enchilada."

Caitlyn smiled as she pointed out something that neither of them had considered. "Remember," she said, "the winner of the Big Enchilada makes it on the plaque, too."

Meanwhile, Shane was standing next to the boys from Connect Three.

"This time *you're* going down, Shane," Jason warned.

"Don't forget boys," Shane reminded them, "I've won the Big Enchilada before. This will be a walk in the park."

"You were lucky that time," Nate chimed in. "This time, you are finishing behind both of us."

Shane just smiled and got into position. "We'll see about that."

"Is everybody ready?" Brown called out.

"Ready!" they all replied.

Brown smiled for a moment and then signaled the race to begin. As soon as he yelled, "Go!" the campers raced across a large, muddy field called Muddy Waters in honor of the great blues musician.

"This is so gross," Mitchie said gleefully as she sank calf deep into the gooey mud.

The campers who tried to go fast slipped and slid, while the ones who went slowly sank deeper and deeper into the muck.

The surprise leader of the pack was Tess. She had figured out a strategy that had eluded the others. Everyone was going to get covered in mud, she realized. The trick was not caring. If you tried to keep from getting muddy, it only added to your time. Keeping clean wasn't an option. So she dropped down on her hands and knees and scampered right through the field. She had mud all over her, but she was the first one to make it out. Observing her success, Caitlyn and Shane quickly did the same and were soon close behind her.

The second task in the obstacle course was

called Jumping Jack Flash and was named in honor of the hit Rolling Stones song. Each camper had to do forty-seven jumping jacks, one for each year the Stones had been together.

Tess might not have liked sports, but she did like going to the gym and working out with her mom, so the jumping jacks were no problem for her. A bonus was that most of the mud fell off her as she did them. By the time she was done, all of the big clumps were gone.

Mitchie had finally made it out of the mud. By the time she made it to the jumping jacks, she was running even with Jason and Nate.

"How are you holding up?" Caitlyn asked as she finished her last jumping jack.

"I'm hoping there's a break sometime soon," Mitchie joked.

"You're going to have to go faster," Shane said teasingly to Jason and Nate. "I'm moving on, and you just got here."

Tess was still in the lead when she reached the third task, a jog around the camp called the Long and Winding Road, after a Beatles song. She was trying not to get excited but couldn't help thinking about how much fun it would be to win the race.

Meanwhile, Caitlyn and Shane were closing in behind her. "Who's ahead of us?" Shane asked as they jogged along the path.

"Just Tess, I think," Caitlyn said.

Both of them smiled and picked up their pace.

The fourth stop was at the camp's archery range and was called Bow and Aerosmith. Each camper had to shoot at a target until he or she made a bull's-eye.

For the first time since the race had begun, Tess felt a shiver of doubt. Her lead became tenuous and then gone. Caitlyn and Shane both reached the range while she was still shooting.

None of them, however, was having much

luck at the challenge. They were still going a few minutes later when Mitchie arrived, followed closely by Nate and Jason.

Mitchie had never been great at archery. But, amazingly, she hit a bull's-eye on her very first attempt.

She let out a squeal and started to run toward the lake where the last two stops were located. Just like that, she had taken the lead.

A few seconds later, Tess hit a bull's-eye and was right behind her. The two girls who had most dreaded Sound Off were now neck-and-neck for the lead in the biggest event of all.

As they ran to the lake, they both laughed.

"This is so ridiculous," Mitchie said.

"Ridiculous and fun," Tess added.

The fifth task of the course was named after a Simon and Garfunkel song called "Bridge Over Troubled Water." There was a bridge made of barrels across a corner of the lake. It bobbed up and down whenever anyone crossed it. When there were a lot of people on it, it bobbed all over the place.

Mitchie was the first one to make it to the bridge, although Tess was close behind her. They looked ahead and saw that after the bridge all they had to do was run down the dock and jump off the end into the water. It was certain that one of the two of them would win.

Mitchie was about halfway across the bridge when it suddenly bobbed up.

"Hold on!" Tess warned her. But it was too late.

Mitchie lost her balance. She tried to catch herself, but all she managed to do was wave her arms wildly. She fell into the lake with a loud splash.

Tess had it in the bag.

Until . . . she stopped and went back to help Mitchie.

"Give me your hand," she said, kneeling down to reach for her.

"What are you doing?" Mitchie cried. "You can win this."

Tess simply reached out for her again. "Give me your hand," she said. "Leaving someone behind is so un-Vibe-like."

Reaching up out of the water, Mitchie smiled as Tess pulled her back onto the bridge. Just as Mitchie was about to climb all the way back on, the next wave of racers reached the bridge and caused it to bob up and down.

Within seconds, Tess and Mitchie flew off the bridge and back into the water. They were underwater for a few seconds, but when they got back to the surface, both of them were laughing.

"At least this should get the rest of the mud off," Tess joked.

"I can't believe you came back for me," Mitchie said. While they were in the water, a large group of people started to pass them. The leader was Shane. When he saw Mitchie and Tess, he slowed down to make sure they were all right.

"Gotcha!" Jason said as he sprinted past Shane. "This year I'm going to win."

Jason and Nate both gleefully turned down the dock and ran to the end. They jumped off side by side and hit the water at the same time.

"I won!" Jason shouted, his mouth full of water as he returned to the surface.

"You did not," Nate answered. "I won!"

"No you didn't," a voice called out to them.

They turned to face Caitlyn, Lorraine, and Ella. The voice belonged to Ella.

"She won," Ella said, pointing at Caitlyn.

Jason and Nate had been so focused on Shane that they hadn't noticed that the girls had already passed him.

"Lorraine came in second," she added. "And I came in third."

The three girls smiled happily at their sweep of the top spots.

"But fourth is good," Caitlyn said with a big smile.

Sound Off had been a huge success. While the events had not followed Caitlyn's plans exactly, they certainly had in spirit. And, though the Vibe team did not finish at the top of the pack, the four girls who made up the team had not only had fun, but also become much better friends.

It had been a day filled with surprises, but perhaps none bigger than what occurred at that night's awards celebration.

Right after Caitlyn received her award for winning the Big Enchilada—a real giant enchilada, prepared especially for her by Connie—the Golden Drumstick was given out.

"This award," Brown said, "is given to the camper who has shown the most spirit and best sportsmanship. And this year, it is my great honor to give it to Tess Tyler."

As Tess stood there in total shock, her teammates hooted and hollered. They might not have won the big events, but their prize was much sweeter. They had figured out how to work together and, better still, be friendly to one another.

Mitchie smiled as she looked around the room. Once again, Camp Rock had given her a day to remember.

Keep rockin' with another all-new
story from camp!

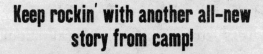

SECOND
SESSION
#7

Stage Fright

By N.B. Grace

Based on "Camp Rock," Written by Karin Gist & Regina Hicks and Julie Brown & Paul Brown

"**H**ey, mom, what's cookin'?" Mitchie Torres asked as she dashed into the Camp Rock kitchen.

Her mother, Connie, turned from the stove

and grinned at her daughter. "No matter how many times I hear that joke, it never gets old," she said drily. "It's truly amazing."

Mitchie laughed. "I know it's an oldie—but you gotta admit, it's a goody!" She danced over to the refrigerator, her dark brown hair bouncing, and took out a carton of orange juice. As she poured herself a glass, she hummed softly to herself.

She could still hardly believe that she was lucky enough to attend Camp Rock. And when she thought about all the good friends she'd made over the past two sessions— Caitlyn, Peggy, Lola, and Shane—she felt even luckier.

Her spirits were especially high today, because it was a picture-perfect summer morning. The sun was warm, but a cool breeze kept the temperature down. The sky was cloudless and a brilliant blue. Birds were singing cheerfully in the trees. *In fact . . .*

Mitchie cocked her head to listen more

closely. It wasn't just birds singing! A few campers who had already finished breakfast were hanging out in the B-Note canteen, practicing a song a cappella. Mitchie nodded to herself as she listened. It's hard to sing without any musical accompaniment and sound good . . . and these singers sounded really good.

Curious, she pushed the kitchen door open and peeked into the dining area. Three girls sitting at a nearby table were the singers. They could have been triplets, Mitchie thought. All three had ponytails (although two of the ponytails were brown and one was blond); all three were wearing identical khaki shorts and white T-shirts; and all three swayed to the beat of the music in a synchronized fashion. As they finished their song, there was a light round of applause from the other campers in the mess hall.

Barron James yelled, "Awesome job, Torie!" The girl with the blond ponytail smiled and waved a hand in acknowledgment, then said to the other two, "We nailed that one, guys. Do you want to practice 'Sitting on the Dock of the Bay' now?"

Her friends nodded.

"Great," Torie said. "Follow me. . . ."

As they began crooning the classic Otis Redding song, Mitchie closed the door.

"I guess we got some new campers," she said.

Her mother squirted some soap into the sink full of hot water. "Yes, I heard Brown talking about that last night," Connie said as she plunged a dirty pan into the sink. "Or maybe I should say, I heard him groovin' to an extremely enthusiastic beat about how cool it was that he could arrange for some kids to arrive a few days late for the session."

Mitchie grinned at her mother's wry tone. Brown Cesario, the director of Camp Rock, had retired from a long career in the music business to become the director of Camp

Rock and his high spirits and abundant energy kept the place rockin'. Not to mention his endless tales of musicians he had known and his unique way of working music into any conversation.

"Well, it doesn't sound like they'll have a hard time catching up," Mitchie observed, nodding toward the canteen where the girls were finishing up with some smooth and soulful vocals. "Hey, do you need some help with drying?"

"Thanks, honey," Connie said with a grateful smile. "But you need to eat your breakfast first. You know, breakfast is—"

"The most important meal of the day. I know, I know!" Mitchie finished her mother's sentence. "Okay, let me finish my nutritious breakfast, and then I'll have the energy I need to come back in here and help out."

A few minutes later, Mitchie had filled her plate with scrambled eggs. As she was nabbing a slice of toast, she looked around the canteen for a seat.

Her best friend, Caitlyn Gellar, was nowhere to be seen. Mitchie grinned to herself. Bunking in the same cabin, Mitchie had discovered that Caitlyn was a real night owl who loved to stay up late talking or practicing the guitar or learning a new song. Last night, she'd been reading a new novel that she said she just couldn't put down. Even as Mitchie had drifted off to sleep, Caitlyn's mini reading light was still glowing. Mitchie had a feeling that her friend was probably willing to miss breakfast—despite its *obvious* importance!—in order to get a little extra sleep.

As Mitchie's eyes continued to scan the room, a hint of disappointment clouded her good mood. When she stopped to figure out what had caused the dip in her spirits, she realized that she'd been hoping not to see just Caitlyn. She had also been hoping to see Shane Gray.

Not that she didn't see quite a lot of him. In fact, she still couldn't believe that she was friends with the lead singer of the famous band Connect Three. He also happened to be Brown's nephew. But then again Camp Rock had been nothing if not surprising. Their friendship was another amazing thing that had happened to her here.

Even though Shane wasn't in the canteen, she was certain to see him later. Right now, she had to hurry up and eat so that she could go help her mom. Mitchie took a seat in a secluded corner, where she was half hidden behind a rolling equipment trunk that had been wheeled into the canteen for that afternoon's acoustic set. She realized that she was actually pleased to have a little time to herself so she could think about something that had been troubling her.

She had been working on a song all week. It had started off well, but then she got stuck after finishing one verse. Every line she had written seemed forced. Every note she tried sounded false.

Part of her knew that she should put the song aside and work on something else. Often, when she did that, she came back to the problem song and found that the solution was obvious, as if her mind had been working on it while she was busily thinking other thoughts.

But she felt *so close* to figuring out how to write this song! She didn't want to give up. She couldn't. Mitchie felt as if the song already existed somewhere just beyond her grasp, shimmering in the future. If only she could reach out and grab it . . .

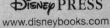